Paul Bunyan

A long time ago, there was a baby so big that it took not one, but five storks to deliver him to his parents! The arrival of the big baby caused quite a stir in the small coastal Maine town, for no one had ever seen a baby of such an epic size before!

The baby's proud parents named him Paul Bunyan. Now it is true that babies grow quickly, but Paul grew faster than any baby! He was always hungry and ate a huge amount of food. After just one week, Paul was so large that he was already wearing his father's clothes!

One night, when the ocean was peaceful and everyone in the town was nestled snugly in their beds, Paul drifted off to sleep, too. Unfortunately, Paul moved around quite a bit in his sleep. In fact, he rolled around in his sleep so many times that night he caused an earthquake!

The people of the town moaned and groaned. It seemed like Paul was always disturbing the peace somehow, even when he did regular things that everyone did! And it was all on account of his huge size!

"This just won't do!" cried the townspeople. "Paul has to go!"

Paul had grown to be so big that his parents didn't know what to do with him. And so, Paul's parents gathered up their things and took Paul deep into the woods, and that is where Paul grew up.

From a young age, Paul could do many things that boys his age didn't, or couldn't, do very well. One of these things was wielding an ax. Because of his unusually large size, cutting down trees was easy for Paul! With one swift chop, he could take out several trees at once!

By the time Paul was about twenty, he had the strength of fifty men. He grew restless, and decided that it was time to move west and seek new adventure. He said goodbye to his parents, and with his ax over his shoulder, he set off on his own.

As Paul continued west, he encountered the most terrible snowstorm anyone had witnessed in ages. A dreadful chill crept across the land, and Paul found it harder and harder to carry on.

Paul trudged along through the swirling snow, so thick he could hardly see. He found shelter in a spot of the woods where the trees were thick and built a fire. As he warmed himself by the fire, he heard a strange cry: "Maa! Maa!"

What could that be? wondered Paul.

He followed the sound, making his way through snowdrifts, until at last he came upon a large animal frozen in the snow. It was certainly no ordinary animal: it was giant, blue baby ox! Paul bent down and picked up the ox. He carried him back to the fire to warm up.

Paul and the blue ox became fast friends. Paul named him Babe. The two were inseparable! Babe continued to grow, and before long, the horns on his head reached the top of the tallest trees.

One day, Paul cut down trees with his trusty ax for the people in a nearby town. They needed the lumber to build all sorts of things, like new houses, buildings, and barns for the growing population.
Babe helped him with the work by rolling the logs to the river so they could float down to the sawmill.

This gave Paul an idea: he and Babe could be traveling lumberjacks! That way, they could see the country and help out people along the way. And they were already a great team!

When they arrived at their first logging camp, the lumberjacks were certainly surprised! They had never seen such a giant man and ox before!

At first, people were afraid because Paul and Babe were so large, but as they moved from forest to forest, and from town to town, the gentle giants became the most famous lumberjack team in the land. Everywhere they went, they performed good deeds and helped people along the way.

One time, Paul caught hundreds of fish with his bare hands and delivered them all to the cook at a local lumber camp. Everyone was so pleased! The fish fed the lumberjacks for weeks!

Another time, with one stomp on the ground with his giant hoof, Babe made a public pool for a town to enjoy during the hot summer days. Paul and Babe's good deeds were endless!

As they neared the end of their traveling days, Babe grew tired and thirsty, so Paul dug out the Great Lakes to provide him with drinking water. Then, Paul turned to Babe and said: "It's time to settle down, Babe. Where shall we make our home?"

That's when they settled on the edge of the Big Onion River in Minnesota, and started their very own logging company.

Paul spread the word that they were looking for lumberjacks to work at the logging camp. Thousands of men traveled from far and wide for the chance to work with Paul and Babe. Paul hired hundreds of lumberjacks, but the men he liked to work with the best were the biggest and strongest of the bunch. They came to be known as the Seven Axmen, and each was named Elmer so that when Paul called their name, they would all come running at once.

Lucy the Purple Cow produced all of the camp's dairy products. The camp's cook, Sourdough Sam, used her milk, among other ingredients, to make his logging camp specialty: pancakes. The lumberjacks were very hungry men who could eat dozens of pancakes in just one sitting!

They had such large appetites and ate so much that something had to be done! Paul turned to Ole Olafson, the master blacksmith, who had specially crafted Babe's giant shoes. Ole made a giant iron griddle so that Sam could cook a whole bunch of pancakes at once to fill all the hungry lumberjacks' bellies.

Paul and Babe's logging company lasted for many, many years. It became the biggest logging camp in the land! But it was not without a few snags along the way. Mosquitoes were a problem at the camp. The lumberjacks were getting bitten all over! Paul had to do something.

Paul thought that a good solution would be to bring in big bees to chase the mosquitoes away, but when the bees and the mosquitoes married each other, the problem only got worse!

One day, the bees and mosquitoes noticed a sugar boat that was bringing sugar to the camp. They swarmed the boat and became so full from all the sugar they ate that they couldn't fly anymore and drowned in the river! Paul managed to save two mosquitoes, who began to help the lumberjacks by drilling holes in the maple trees so that the lumberjacks could have maple syrup on their pancakes.

Now the lumber company is gone, but what about Paul and Babe? Their legend lives on. If you listen very carefully the next time you're in the woods, you just may hear Paul's far-off call: "Tim-ber!"